Christm

for kias!

By Silly Billy

Q: Why is Christmas just like your job?

A: You do all the work and the fat guy with the suit gets all the credit.

Q: What's the difference between the Christmas alphabet and the ordinary alphabet?

A: The Christmas alphabet has Noel.

Q: What do you call people who are afraid of Santa Claus?

A: Claustrophobic.

Q: What's brown and sneaks round the kitchen?

A: Mince spies.

Q: Why can't the Christmas tree stand up?

A: It doesn't have legs.

Q: What do you call an obnoxious reindeer?

A: RUDEolph.

Q: What nationality is Santa Claus?

A: North Polish.

Q: Why was Santa's little helper depressed?

A: Because he had low elf esteem.

Q: What do you call a kid who doesn't believe in Santa?

A rebel without a Claus.

Q: What do you get when you cross a bell with a skunk?

A: Jingle smells.

Q: Why does Santa have three gardens?

A: So he can ho-ho-ho!

Q: How much did Santa pay for his sleigh?

A: Nothing, it was on the house!

Q: What's red and white and gives presents to good little fish on Christmas?

A: Sandy Claws.

Q: What do you get when you cross a snowman with a vampire?

A: Frostbite.

Q: What do you call an elf who sings?

A: A wrapper!

Q: What do you get when you cross an archer with a gift-wrapper?

A: Ribbon hood.

Q: What do you get when you combine a Christmas tree with an iPad?

A: A pineapple!

Q: What did Adam say on the day before Christmas?

A: "It's Christmas, Eve!"

Q. What do you get if you cross mistletoe and a duck?

A. A Christmas Quacker.

Q. What do call Santa when he stops moving?

A. Santa Pause!

Q. Where does a snowman keep his money?

A. In a snow bank.

Q: What does Mrs Claus say to Santa when she sees clouds?

A: Looks like rain, dear

Q. Why do mummies like Christmas so much?

A. Because of all the wrapping!

Q: What do zombies put on their Christmas turkey?

A: Grave-y

Knock knock

Who's there?

Mary!

Mary who?

Merry Christmas

Knock, knock

Who's there?

Chris!

Chris who?

Christmas!!!!

Q: What do you call Frosty the Snowman in May?

A: A puddle!

Q: Where do reindeer go to dance?

A: Christmas balls!

Q: What's red, white and blue at Christmas time?

A: A sad candy cane!

Q: What did Mary Poppins want from Santa?

A: Supercalifragilistic-expialisnowshoes!

Q: An honest politician, a kind lawyer and Santa Claus were talking when they all noticed a $5 bill on the floor. Who picked it up?

A: Santa of course, the other two don't exist!

Knock Knock,

Who's there?

Hanna!

Hanna who?

Hanna partridge in a pear tree!

Q: What does Santa say at the start of a race?

A: Ready, set, Ho! Ho! Ho!"

Knock, knock.

Who's there?

Murray.

Murray who?

Murray Christmas, one and all!

Q: What's a good time for Santa to come down the chimney?

A: Anytime!

Q: What do snowmen like to do on the weekend?

A: Chill out.

Q: What does Jack Frost like best about school?

A: Snow and tell.

Q: What do snowmen eat for breakfast?

Ice Crispies.

Moe: What are you going to give your little brother for Christmas this year?

Joe: I haven't decided yet.

Moe: What did you give him last year?

Joe: The measles.

Teacher: Johnny, define claustrophobia.

Johnny: Fear of Santa Claus?

Knock, knock.

Who's there?

Olive.

Olive, who?

Olive the other reindeer.

Q: What do elves do after school?

A: Their gnome work!

Q: What's white and red and goes up and down and up and down?

A: Santa Claus in an elevator!

Q: What's the difference between Santa's reindeer and a knight?

A: One slays the dragon, and the other's draggin' the sleigh.

When asked about his job, Frosty always replies, "There's no business like snow business."

Knock, knock!

Who's there?

Dexter.

Dexter, who?

Dexter halls with boughs of holly.

Q: What do you get when you cross a snowman and a dog?

A: Frostbite.

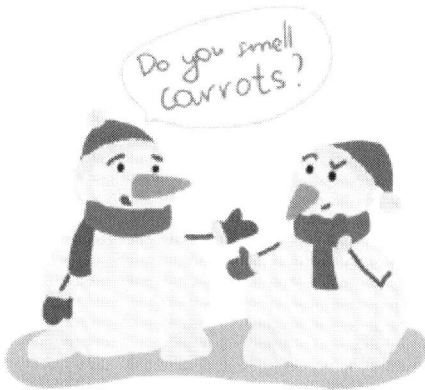

Q: What did one snowman say to the other snowman?

A: Do you smell carrots?

One night a Viking named Rudolph the Red was looking out the window when he said, "It's going to rain."

His wife asked, "How do you know?"

"Because Rudolph the Red knows rain, dear."

Q: What's white and goes up?

A: A confused snowflake!

Q: What do you call an old snowman?

A: Water!

Q: What do you sing at a snowman's birthday party?

A: Freeze a jolly good fellow!

Q: What goes: "Now you see me, now you don't, now you see me, now you don't?"

A: A snowman on a zebra crossing!

Q: What goes ho-ho whoosh, ho-ho whoosh?

A: Santa caught in a revolving door!

Q: What goes "oh, oh, oh"?

A: Santa walking backwards!

Knock knock!

Who's there?

Snow.

Snow who?

Snow use – I've forgotten my name again!

Q: When does Christmas come before Thanksgiving?

A: In the dictionary!

Q: Who delivers presents to baby sharks at Christmas?

A: Santa Jaws!

Q: What do you have in December that's not in any other month?

A: The letter D!

Q: Why is it always cold at Christmas?

A: Because it's in Decemberrrr!

Q: What Christmas carol is a favorite of parents?

A: Silent Night!

Q: What's impossible to overtake at Christmas?

A: The three wide men!

Q: How does a snowman lose weight?

A: He waits for the weather to get warmer!

Q: What do snowmen eat for breakfast?

A: Frosted flakes!

Q: Where do snowmen go to dance?

A: A snowball!

Q: How many presents can Santa fit in an empty sack?

A: Only one, after that it's not empty any more!

Q: What do you get if you eat Christmas decorations?

A: Tinselitus!

Q: What carol is heard in the desert?

A: Camel ye faithful!

Q: What do monkeys sing at Christmas?

A: Jungle bells, jungle bells!

Q: What does a cat on the beach have in common with Christmas?

A: Sandy claws!

Q: What is Santa's dog called?

A: Santa Paws!

Q: What do you get if you cross Santa Claus with a detective?

A: Santa Clues!

Q: What do you get if Santa goes down the chimney when the fire is lit?

A: Crisp Cringle!

Q: Why did Santa get a ticket on Christmas Eve?

A: He left his sleigh in a *snow* parking zone.

Q: What do you call Santa Claus when he doesn't move?

A: Santa Pause!

Q: How do sheep greet each other at Christmas?

A: A merry Christmas to ewe!

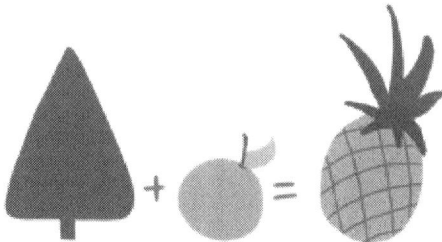

Q: What do you get if you cross an apple with a Christmas tree?

A: A pineapple!

Q: What kind of candle burns longer, a red candle or a green candle?

A: Neither, candles always burn shorter!

Q: What happened to the man who shoplifted a calendar at Christmas?
A: He got 12 months!

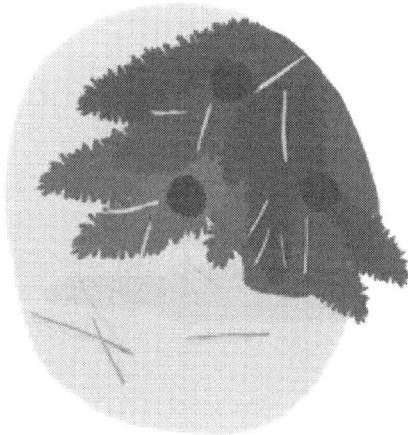

Q: Why are Christmas trees like bad knitters?
A: They both drop needles!

Q: What often falls at the North Pole but never gets hurt?

A: Snow!

Q: What is the best Christmas present in the world?

A: A broken drum – you can't beat it!

Q: What do you call Santa's helpers?

A: Subordinate Clauses.

Q: What's a good Christmas tip?

A: Never catch snowflakes with your tongue until all the birds have gone south for the winter.

Q: What did the big angel say to the little angel on Christmas Eve?

A: Halo there!

Q: How do you know that Santa is a man?

A: No woman wears the same attire every year.

Q: What a big candle says to a small candle on a Christmas Eve?

A: I am going out for dinner tonight.

Q: What does Tarzan sing at Christmas?

A: Jungle Bells.

Q: What snowmen wear on the Christmas Eve?

A: Ice caps.

Q: What kind of motorbike does Santa ride?

A: A Holly Davidson!

Q: Who is Santa's favorite singer?

A: Elf-is Presley!

Q: What is someone who claps on Christmas Eve called?

A: Santapplause!

Q: Why is it getting harder to buy Advent calendars?

A: Because their days are numbered!

Q: Cinderella was a poor football player - Do you know the reason?

A: She used to run away from the ball.

Q: Name a child's favorite Christmas king?

A: A stocking.

Q: On Christmas morning the cowboy said what?

A: Mooooey Christmas.

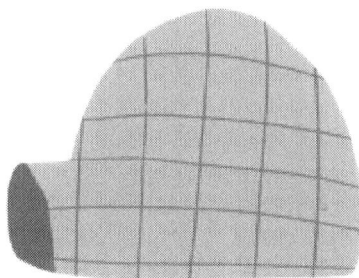

Q: What do you all know about *ig*?

A: An Eskimo house without a Loo.

Q: How does a yeti get down from the hilltop?

A: By-icicle.

Q: Who delivers Christmas presents to elephants?

A: Elephanta Claus

Q: What for the trumpet of Ken was kept in the freezer?

A: Because he loves cool music.

Q: What could be a perfect gift for the station master during Christmas?

A: Platform Shoes.

Q: Did you know Santa had only eight reindeer last Christmas?

A: Comet stayed home to clean the sink.

Q: What is the popular carol in Desert?

A: Camel ye Faithful.

Q: What's red and white, red and white, red and white?

A: Santa Claus rolling down the hill.

Q: Why did the elves ask the turkey to join the band?

A: Because he had the drumsticks.

Q: What did the Christmas tree say to the ornament?

A: Aren't you tired of just hanging around?

Q: What goes "oh, oh, oh"?

A: Santa walking backwards.

Q: What's Santa's favorite sandwich?

A: Peanut butter and jolly!

Q. What is green, white, and red all over?

A. A sunburned elf

Q. What never eats at Christmas dinner?

A. The turkey – it's stuffed

Q: Did you hear about Dracula's Christmas party?

A: It was a scream

25177370R00032

Printed in Great Britain
by Amazon